BOBS AND Tweets
Scout Camp!

by PEPPER SPRINGFIELD

illustrated by KRISTY CALDWELL

SCHOLASTIC INC.

Dedicated to Maggie Anderson
–PS

For David
–KC

All rights reserved. Published by Scholastic Inc., *Publishers since 1920*. SCHOLASTIC and associated logos are trademarks and/or registered trademarks of Scholastic Inc.

The publisher does not have any control over and does not assume any responsibility for author or third-party websites or their content.

No part of this publication may be reproduced, stored in a retrieval system, or transmitted in any form or by any means, electronic, mechanical, photocopying, recording, or otherwise, without written permission of the publisher. For information regarding permission, write to Scholastic Inc., Attention: Permissions Department, 557 Broadway, New York, NY 10012.

This book is a work of fiction. Names, characters, places, and incidents are either the product of the author's imagination or are used fictitiously, and any resemblance to actual persons, living or dead, business establishments, events, or locales is entirely coincidental.

ISBN 978-1-338-35540-6

10 9 8 7 6 5 4 3 2   20 21 22 23

Printed in the U.S.A.   40
First edition, September 2019

Book design: Becky James
Color Flatter: Mike Freiheit

TABLE OF CONTENTS

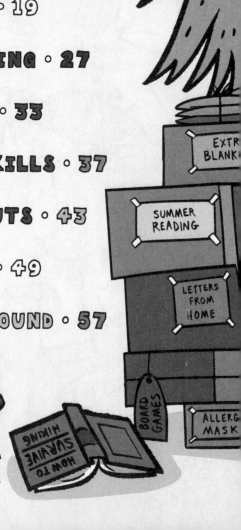

CHAPTER 1
NO BOBS ON BOARD

"Dean!" six Bobs yell. "Whoop! Whoop! Hold the bus.

"We want to come with you. Make room for us."

"No Bobs!" groans Dean from his seat next to Lou.

"Scout Camp is for kids. There is no room for you."

"At Scout Camp we hike. Pitch tents and canoe.
We challenge ourselves. Prove what *we* can do."

"At camp," Lou chimes in, "we survive on our own."
"Sit down! Buckle up," calls out Bus Driver Joan.
Ms. Pat blows her whistle. "Scouts, wave good-bye."
"Please, Bobs!" begs Dean. "There is no need to cry."

The bus trip is long. They make a pit stop.

Ramona and Sal look for a gift shop.

Zach stays on board. He wants to keep reading.

"Ms. Pat!" Sherman yells. "Chucky P.'s nose is bleeding."

Bus Driver Joan turns down the ramp.

"Look, Lou," says Dean, "the signs for Scout Camp."

"A forest!" cries Lou. "Those pine trees are tall.

And look over there—a huge waterfall."

SCOUT CAMP

CHAPTER 2
THIS IS CAMP

"Bonefish Scouts!" says Ms. Pat. "At last, we are here.

Get off the bus. Collect all your gear.

Follow me down to the bunks to unpack."

"I have bear spray," says Sal, "in case grizzlies attack."

"Mr. Bigtree," whines Sherman, "is this a tick?"

"Lifeguard Mark," moans Samir, "I am homesick."

"*Are you kidding?*" Zach groans. "Top bunks make me dizzy."

"Stop whining," says Mark, "unpack, let's get busy."

Dean makes his bunk, then goes to find Lou.
"I am happy to be here at Scout Camp with you."
"Me too," says Lou, "we can do things *our* way.
No Bobs and Tweets fighting to mess up our day."

Ms. Pat blows her whistle. "Scouts, time for lunch.
There is mail for Lou—in fact, quite a bunch."
"It figures," sighs Lou. "Supplies for a year!"
"My Tweets are convinced I cannot survive here."

CHAPTER 3
HIKE WITH MIKE

Chef Mo serves a picnic of tacos and beans.
Chucky spills salsa all over his jeans.
A man joins the group. "I am Scout Leader Mike.
Welcome to Camp! Are you ready to hike?"

"Hike?" groans Zach. "*Are you kidding me?*
I choose to stay here and read by this tree.
My ankle is sore. It is allergy weather."
"No, Zach," says Mike, "all Scouts hike together."

"Come on, Zach," says Lou. "I know how you feel.
I used to hate hiking. Now I like it, for real.
My Tweets make up songs and dance moves as we hike.
I will teach you some fun songs I think you will like."

Dean holds out a hand. He pulls Zach to his feet.
"Lou, teach us," Dean cries, "to hike like a Tweet."

TRAIL TO
THE PEAK

Lou, Dean, and Zach sing as they climb.
They have so much fun, they lose track of time.
Mike shows them ferns. And brown trout in the creek.
He lets Zach plant the flag when they get to the peak.

"Bonefish Scouts," exclaims Mike, "check out the view.
Mother Nature created all this for you."

They drink from canteens. They share Mo's trail mix.
Scout Leader Mike helps them find walking sticks.
They hike back down. The Scouts sing all the way.
"Thanks to you, Lou," Zach grins, "that hike was okay."

CHAPTER 4
TIPPY TEST

Water safety is next. They head to the lake.

Mark shows them the swim test all Scouts have to take.

"Oh, no!" Brea sobs, "I lost my swimsuit."

"Don't cry," offers Mo. "Try a nice piece of fruit."

"Find a buddy," says Mark, "and choose a canoe.
If it tips, you need to learn what to do.
Paddle out. Flip your boat. Then climb back in."
"Are you kidding?" groans Zach. "I see a shark fin."

"No sharks in this lake. Don't you worry," says Mark.
But, come on, let's get tipping before it gets dark."
The Scouts are paired up. Chucky P. stands alone.
So, he gets to be buddies with Bus Driver Joan.

The Scouts start to paddle. Ramona complains.
"What are we going to do if it rains?"
"Who cares?" says Brea. "We are wet anyway.
Plus, it is pretty sunny today."

Lou and Dean paddle out in their purple canoe.

"I got this one," says Dean. "I know what to do.

My Bobs love water sports. They make their boats tip.

I had to learn a *Bob-Overboard Flip*."

Dean shows the Scouts how to flip their canoes.
"Dean: the Tippy Test Champ. Our hero!" cries Lou.

"Let's tell Mark we are ready for white-water rafting."
"Not me," says Dean. "I would rather try crafting."

CHAPTER 5
TEAM BUILDING

They dine by the campfire, sing songs, make s'mores.

"I like camp," says Sal. "We don't have to do chores."

"Tomorrow," says Mike, "you survive in the wild."

"*Are you kidding?*" groans Zach. "I am just a *child*."

"You are sorted," says Mike, "into Teams Red and Blue.
We have high expectations for each one of you.
Pitch a tent. Light a fire. Spot animal tracks.
Make drinking water. Then find your way back.

You earn badges for each task you complete.

Team captains keep score on these tally sheets."

"Scouts," adds Mike, "you must work together."

"Let's hope," frets Ramona, "that we have good weather."

"Team captains," says Mark, "are Dean Bob and Lou.
Dean Bob for Team Red. Lou Tweet for Team Blue.
Dean and Lou were helpful to all kids today.
They acted like leaders, the Bonefish Scout Way."

The captains are proud, but of course they don't brag.
Mr. Bigtree plays taps. Samir lowers the flag.

"Team Blue," Lou shouts, "come here, huddle in."
"Uh-oh," Dean thinks, "Lou is playing to win."

CHAPTER 6
POWER TRIP

At daybreak Lou bellows, "Blues! Out of bed.

When it comes to Surviving: Team Blue will beat Red.

I made these cool 'Team Blue' baseball caps.

Warm up! Do ten push-ups! Run two full laps."

The Scouts eat Mo's breakfast of bacon and eggs.

"Blues," barks Lou, "come on, work those legs."

"Are you kidding?" Zach whispers. "What's got into Lou?

Thankfully, Dean, I'm on Team Red with you."

Mike leads the Scouts to the survival site.
Chucky P. lags behind. Dean asks, "Are you alright?"
"Keep up!" cries Ramona. "Chucky, walk faster.
Getting lost if a storm comes will be a disaster."

Team Blue runs ahead. They wait for no one.
"Dean," complains Zach, "this is not so much fun.
Ramona keeps stressing about the weather.
And nobody seems to be working together."

They see a crude sign that feels kind of mean.
"Being a captain is hard," mutters Dean.

CHAPTER 7
SURVIVAL SKILLS

"Scouts," says Mike, "first pitch your tents.
Remember to leave a space for the vents."
The Blue Team is rushing. Lou yells, "We are ready!"
"*Are you kidding?*" cries Zach. "That tent is *not* steady."

"Next," says Mike, "build a fire from scratch.
Find a way to do it without a match.
First get a spark. Then try your best.
To fan a fire in your tinder nest."

"You can rub two sticks together," Mike adds.

"Those clouds," groans Ramona, "look pretty bad.

Lou holds Zach's glasses up to the sun.

"Give them back," shouts Zach. "I can't see anyone."

They boil water. Find bugs. Identify plants.

"I think," says Samir, "those are red fire ants."

They eat packed lunches. Then learn some first aid.

Joan passes out cups of Mo's Own Lemonade.

"We rock!" shouts Lou. "Team Blue is the best."
"I am tired," says Sherman. "I need a rest."

"Come on, teams," calls Dean, "let's clean up this place.
Remember our motto: 'Scouts leave no trace.'"

CHAPTER 8
WE ARE SCOUTS

"Good job, Scouts," says Mike. "Now we head back.
You have learned lots of skills that will keep you on track.
Find your way back to Camp. It should take you one hour.
Work as a team. Unlock your Scout power."

"Let's go, Blues," yells Lou. They speed off in a run.
"Clouds," warns Ramona, "are blocking the sun."
"Listen!" says Chucky. "I hear a rumble.
Are those rocks in an avalanche starting to tumble?"

"Thunder!" booms Ramona. "A big storm is coming.
That is why the crickets are humming."
A huge flash of lightning cracks in the sky.
"Are you kidding?" wails Zach. "I am going to cry."

"Stay calm," says Ramona. "I know what to do."
Zach and I will wait here. You guys go find Team Blue.
We can wait in this cave until the storms pass.
I study weather," she adds. "I learned this in class."

"I see them," cries Chucky, "huddled under that tree.
Captain Dean! Let's go get 'em. Come on, follow me."

Now the Scouts are together, safe in the cave.
Zach twists his ankle. But he tries to be brave.
The storm rages on, but the kids are not scared.
They feel proud to be Scouts who are really prepared.

Lou gives Dean a hug. "I got carried away.
I am sorry for how I acted today.
I want to be on the same team as you.
Can we all be Team Purple—one Team: Red and Blue?"

CHAPTER 9
GO CHUCKY!

The storm passes. They exit. "Where are we?" asks Lou.

"I don't know," says Dean. "I'm not sure what to do."

"You mean we are lost! *Are you kidding?*" groans Zach. "Nobody knows how to get back?"

"I do," says Chucky. "I left breadcrumbs behind.
I painted rocks pink. They are easy to find."
"Thank goodness," says Sherman, "we are so lucky."
The Scouts yell together: "Three Cheers for Chucky!"

Chucky's pink rocks lead them all the way back.
Lou and Dean each have an arm around Zach.
He hobbles a bit but they make it OK.
And as you might guess they sing all the way.

Back at Scout Camp, they find a big scene.

"Bobs! Why are you here? What happened?" cries Dean.

Bob One clears his throat and steps forward to speak.

"We missed all you kids. It was a bleak week."

Tweet One chimes in, "We planned a big outing.
For Bonefish Street folks who want to try scouting.
And hike outdoors, pitch tents, and canoe.
Earn badges. Become Bonefish Scouts just like you."

Mr. Bigtree says, "Folks, Mo will pack you a snack.
But then you all will have to head back.
Scout Camp is for kids to find their own voices.
Learn scouting skills. And make the best choices."

The captains' eyes meet. "Wait a minute," says Lou.
"Teams! Huddle in, Mr. Bigtree, you too.
Our folks and our friends came this long way.
Can we make tomorrow Family Day?

"We can give everyone a tour of Scout Camp.
Explain how Dean is the Tippy Test Champ.
We can demonstrate how we had to survive.
And how Ramona and Chucky kept us alive."

"Our folks," Dean adds, "can meet Scout Leader Mike.
Lou can show everyone how we sing while we hike.
They can watch us get badges. We have stories to share."
"I can show them," says Sal, "how to ward off a bear."

Mr. Bigtree agrees: "Scouts lead the way!
Bonefish Scout Camp will host Family Day."

CHAPTER 10
HOMEWARD BOUND

Family Day was a pretty big hit!

They had a great time, but it did rain a bit.

This last day of camp dawns sunny and bright.

"Look," says Ramona "not a storm cloud in sight."

They take a group photo with Scout leader Mike.

"Remember me Scouts the next time you hike."

"*Are you kidding?* How well do you know me?" cries Zach.

"I just hike to the Bonefish Library and back."

Joan starts up the bus. The Scouts find their seats.
Mo hands out box lunches filled with Camp treats.
Ramona says, "Chucky, let's sit together.
I have so much to share about stormy weather."

"I found it!" cries Brea. "My swimsuit was here."

"I love camp." says Samir. "Can we come back next year?"

"No grizzlies!" says Sal. "The bears stayed away."

"You scared them," says Sherman, "with your bear spray."

Lou moves close to Dean, gives him a high five.
"We hiked. We canoed. We learned to survive.
We spent time in nature with ferns and brown trout.
I am proud to be a Bonefish Street Scout."

"Camp was great," says Dean "just like you said.
Now I want to see Chopper, sleep in my own bed.
I need to do laundry, my clothes are all damp.
My things got pretty soggy at camp."

"We captains," Lou adds, "helped each Scout do their part."
I know now true scouting comes from the heart."

THE END